# The Coal Train

PENELOPE FARMER

# The Coal Train

*Illustrated by*
WILLIAM BIRD

Heinemann : London

*William Heinemann Ltd*
*15 Queen Street, Mayfair, London W1X 8BE*

*London Melbourne Toronto*
*Johannesburg Auckland*


*First published 1977*
*© Penelope Farmer 1977*
*Illustrations © William Heinemann Ltd 1977*
*434 94929 9*

*Printed and bound in Great Britain by*
*Morrison & Gibb Ltd, London and Edinburgh*

From an idea by
William Bird

This is the story of why Lizzie and I and Joe and
Leslie and Lily and our Mum and Dad sat round the
fire at three in the morning in the middle of February
1947 eating cake and drinking tea and laughing, in
between yawns. We are the Dudd family, our Dad
is a train driver. Down at the Rail Depot they laugh
when they hear the name of Driver Dudd. "Isn't that
the bloke that drove the excursion train and forgot
to stop?" they say. But our Dad's not laughing
usually, not with us five kids still at home and no
overtime any more, for they've put him on to shunting down at the depot now. Things were particularly
bad that winter in any case. When the war had
finished more than eighteen months ago, in 1945, we
thought everything was bound to get better fast. But
it didn't. It got much worse, even if there wasn't any
bombing: and even if we did know that boys like my

half-brother Alan, who had to go off to do their national service, would be sitting safely in camp in Germany instead of out somewhere fighting and in danger of their lives. Our food rations got smaller and smaller, while everything that wasn't rationed got scarcer and scarcer. And on top of that, this winter, the one after Dad's little mistake, was the worst one anyone could remember. At least the war had been interesting, you never knew what would happen from one day to the next. Now you knew only too well what would happen and it was all bad, I tell you.

We did our best to make things easier for ourselves. For instance we all grew vegetables—our allotment was on the railway embankment behind our house. But in mid-January and February under heavy snow you can't get much in the way of vegetables; and if we had a few brussels sprouts, picking them in icy weather with the frost eating your fingers is no joke. I know, I had to do it. Some people bred rabbits too, we did in our backyard, keeping them under cover in the back lavatory during the winter. But rabbits don't like the cold weather either, they stop breeding then, so there was none of them to eat. (Not that I ever liked them much even if we did swop with other people—eating Mrs Sprott's Bun seeming less treacherous than eating our own Brenda or Bertie. We've always got much too fond of our rabbits, perhaps we should have tried to stop Lizzie giving them names; but none of us ever did.)

So we were almost always hungry; a slice of bread and dripping for breakfast doesn't last long on a cold morning, especially when you're cold before you go out and the backs of your knees are chapped from the frost as most our knees were then. (Though it was better for me after I went to the grammar and was allowed to wear lisle stockings instead of long socks.) We used to take a baked potato each in our pockets to school to warm our hands on, that was our lunch too. But pretty soon we'd be hungry again, and we were always cold. Everyone was—the whole country was desperately short of coal. In some places they had even had to shut down the power-stations so that there was no electricity. We burned everything we could: potato peelings, apple cores, newspapers, paper bags, cardboard boxes, even old socks; when they came to collect our dustbins they must have been nearly empty. But all this made our house smell horrible, and none of it gave much heat. Oh, it was so cold! Oh, I never want to live through a winter like that again—from January till April it lasted. If that's what it's like in Switzerland each year, you can keep Switzerland; the rich that used to go for skiing holidays there before the war must all have needed their heads examining, if you ask me.

Dad put it this way: in 1944, he said, they used to talk about the darkness before dawn; well, the dawn had come in 1945 with the end of the war, and it had decided it didn't like us much so it had gone away again and here we were still in the middle of the night. He was never cheerful those days, Dad, except the evenings when he came back from watching Rita Hayworth at the Regal and even then he said he shouldn't have gone really, they couldn't afford the tickets. But Mum said if she couldn't spare one and nine out of the housekeeping for a trip to the pictures now and then, she didn't know what the world was coming to, good times or bad, and Dad worked hard enough in all conscience, he deserved it.

Like I said, there were five of us kids at home. Alan my half-brother doesn't count really. He's five years older than me, he'll be in the army for another year. His mum died when he was born. I come next, I'm

Margaret Rose after the princess, only they call me Rosie; they're so proud I'm at the grammar, Mum thinks I'll do something really splendid when I grow up, be Manageress of the International Stores or some such, she means by that, but I think I've got other ideas. Next there's Joe, then Lizzie—after the other princess, Elizabeth. I ought to have been that really as the eldest, but Mum liked Margaret Rose the best. Then Leslie and Lily (after Leslie Howard and Lilli Palmer)—they're twins. We all live at No. 1, Kirtley Villas, Railway Approach, next door to Mrs Buttress at the corner shop.

I'll tell you about Mrs Buttress: we all *hate* her. There isn't a Mr Buttress—he went off to the first war and never came back. Who could blame him, Dad would say, rather death in the trenches than Mrs Buttress any day. If Mum sends one of us kids into the shop to buy something from her she makes us wait till every grown-up has been served whether they come in after us or not. And all the time we're hanging about waiting she shouts things like "Take your hands out of that" or "Get away from there" or "Just you wait till I speak to your ma", in a very threatening tone of voice. We suffer from her particularly, living next door to her. She has a little dog as bad-tempered as she is which is always barking at our cat, and then she comes round and complains about our cat setting him off. We'd have rather used some other shop, but our ration books are registered with her, and besides she has a nephew Albert in the

Black Market and sometimes she can offer an extra bit of this or special piece of that to Mum or Dad or someone else in the street, so no one dares offend her too much. She even gives us kids sweets off the ration occasionally, "just to keep you sweet, dearie," she says with what passes on her as a smile. I'd have preferred to go without her sweets myself, but how could you say no to Leslie and Lily. Everyone hates Mrs Buttress, but everyone still needs her.

Mrs Buttress is the only non-railway person in the whole of Kirtley Villas. Next door to us on the other side lives the foreman of Dad's depot, Mr Marwick. We don't have much to do with him and his family, but we used to hear them all right. He'd had two kids late on and their mum is such a quiet little woman she could hardly cope with them; they bawled all the time, or that's what it sounded like. It was hardly surprising their dad spent most of his spare time down at the Temperance Hall playing billiards. Next door to them is a retired head porter from the local station, Mr Sprott, and his very neat thin wife who is always complaining about the foreman's kids either to him—she'd lie in wait till he came home from work—or else to her other neighbour, a guard's widow and our local gossip, Mrs Hipkin. Next door to her is Dad's best mate, a yard foreman, his eldest daughter is my friend Beryl. You always get a piece of cake to eat in Beryl's house.

I don't know what her mum found to put in it those days, though once when it tasted particularly odd, Beryl said she'd made it with liquid paraffin instead of margarine (that's the stuff Mum gives us when we're constipated). I wished I hadn't eaten it then. But Beryl went on and had a second slice. I suppose that's the way she contrives to be the only fat child in our street.

Their neighbours, the Potters, are our local problem. Eight children, dad an engine cleaner, mostly drunk when he isn't working and sometimes when he is, and a mum who usually slops about in slippers and dressing-gown all day looking miserable; but sometimes she'll dress herself up to the nines, cover herself with lipstick and take herself off for a week or more at a time. They have the welfare round

more often than most of us have the milkman and
their house stinks too, you can smell it going past,
and sometimes Mr and Mrs Potter have fights right
out in the street. Once Mrs Hipkin sent for the
police to separate them. She and Mrs Sprott spend
most of their time complaining about them, that is
when they aren't complaining about the Marwick
children, I'm sure if the Potters weren't there they'd
miss them for that reason.

Next door to them lives a shunter, he has two boys,
Michael and Eric, then there is a bomb site, where
the bomb fell in 1942, then an open space and then a

house all by itself and a bit bigger than the rest where the station-master lives and the station-master's wife with her net curtains and her rose-bushes and her poor little brat Billy who doesn't go to the council schools with the rest of us but to some silly little private school instead wearing a silly little blue cap, a size too small for him. It didn't seem to do him much good, you never saw a more miserable looking boy. I don't think I ever saw him smile even until—until? Well, that's the whole point of this story; of what I am writing.

Like I said; we are all railway. It's hard to forget

that ever, living where we do, right under the main line to Scotland. The trains go past night and day throwing sparks at us. There are the squeaks and clunks and groans of the goods trains coming to a halt and then painfully starting up again. There is the steady drumming of the local passenger trains, and then there is the thunder of the expresses—our whole terrace shakes when an express tears past. You get to know the timing of all of them, but especially of those, the 8.15 to Glasgow, the 10.20 to Edinburgh, and you miss them if they don't come. Once during the war we were evacuated to the country and my ears couldn't make it out at all, straining all the time after non-existent trains; as if taking the trains away had the same effect on my ears as taking one of the colours away would have had on my eyes.

It was the noise in fact that began the famous night. There was snow outside as there had been for weeks and more still was falling. We were all of us sitting in the back kitchen huddled as near to the stove as we could get, and listening to "Much Binding" on the wireless, except for Dad who was flopped in his armchair looking vacant and trying not to hear. What he really liked was Sandy Macpherson playing the theatre organ. Behind was the sound of yet another train, one of those interminable coal trains. I don't suppose any of us noticed it particularly; until Dad said suddenly—and when I turned round I saw him

sitting up alert, listening—"He's coming down too fast." There was a sudden jamming on of brakes, followed by a roar of protest which must have been from the first engine as the steam was forced into reverse, and then the clashes of buffers and the shriek of a whistle.

I'd never seen Dad move so fast. "My God it's a banger and on this track too. Everybody out." I grabbed Lily who was nearest me and next minute we were all in the front room in the dark, terrified.

The noise had become deafening, whistles, banging, crashing, clanging, tearing metal, crushing wood, men shouting dreadful language, they could have been in our front room shouting it at us. Then there was a noise like a rainstorm on top of the house itself. We stood there immobile, petrified.

"It's like the war all over again," said Mum, trembling.

"End of the world more like," said Dad.

The noise was subsiding by now, leaving the odd squeak and groan from wheels running on nothing.

Men were still shouting, but not so wildly. The engines blew their valves, roaring steam. I thought that they must be off the track. Living that close to trains you know just how they ought to sound; you also know how they oughtn't.

"I'll go and see what's happened," Dad said.

Someone remembered to put the light on then. We'd all been standing in the dark like idiots, but then we were still used to the blackout during the war. Dad went out to the back again. We heard him unlatch the back door and then we heard a rushing sound. And almost at once we heard an enormous shout from Dad.

"Crikey! The yard's full of coal."

Somehow he'd got the door shut again and then he was gone, shouting over his shoulder to Mum, "I won't be long. Better start making tea."

Mum looked at the stove and said, "At least we might as well be warm." She opened the air-vent to make the stove burn up, handed the hod to Joe and proceeded to inch the door open slowly while the rest of us watched in amazement.

"Out of my way then." She took the hod and dug it in, more coal tumbling in at the door, and the rest of us picked up odd lumps and threw them into the hod besides.

"It's a return for the rabbits anyway," she said angrily. "I don't doubt they're suffocated out there. Not to mention the brussels sprouts. They owe it us." I couldn't think why she was being so fierce about it.

Afterwards between us we forced the door to. Meanwhile Mum had filled up the stove, and sending Joe to fetch the coal scuttle, she filled that up as well, and then marched off with it into the front room.

"Wash your hands all of you," she called back. "To look at you anyone would think this was a coal mine. And Rosie, sweep the coal dust up off the floor if you don't mind. Your Dad'll be bringing people back if I know him, and even if we are warm, it's no excuse not to be decent. Just let's hope there's no one killed."

Lizzie tugged at me afterwards. "Rosie, I'm going upstairs to look out of the back window, we might be able to see it, what's happened. We'll be able to see something."

"If Mum doesn't have another job for us." But she was kneeling on the floor with her back to us holding up a newspaper to make the fire draw, and didn't even see us go past.

It had stopped snowing outside. When our eyes got used to the dark we could see the embankment and the sky above it. We could see trucks tumbled along the line and down the banks, looking like the toy ones Alan used to have before the war. We could even see the coal in the light of a couple of lamps out there. It was as if our yard and all the yards we could see had been turned into coal bunkers. As for the allotments on the embankment, they were buried completely.

"No more cabbage then," said Lizzie, with satisfaction.

"No more sprouts either," I said. "That's not so good."

"I don't like sprouts."

"Nor do I like sprouts," said Lily who'd come up with us, followed by Leslie. He was her shadow always, a little runt of a boy you'd think to look at him, though he had quite a mind of his own when he chose to.

"I like them when I don't have to pick them," I said.

"So do I," said Leslie. And then: "Do you think anyone was killed?"

"The back of the train's still standing so the Tailend Charlie'd be all right," I said. Tailend Charlie is what railmen call the guard.

"How about the drivers and firemen then?"

"How should I know if I can't see them? But it looks like the engines aren't turned over." There was a light bobbing up there along the track; no, two lights, two men. I wondered if one of them was Dad. Two years ago, a year ago, one of those men on the footplate we were talking about, might have been him. He might have been the driver. This didn't seem to have occurred to any of the others.

"Dead as a doornail. Squashed," said Leslie, with what sounded almost like satisfaction.

"Do you mind. That's people you're talking about. People like our Dad."

Yet the trucks looked unreal, like toys. You wouldn't believe seeing them spilled and smashed so lightly how solid and heavy they are. When you see them normally, you wouldn't think even a giant could break them. And now. . . .

"Isn't that Mrs Sprott out there?" said Lizzie (Mrs Sprott who always thought herself better than the rest of us). Her yard didn't look quite as full as ours, at any rate there she was, she'd got her door open and was standing out there peering up at the windows above her. After a minute she bent down and we distinctly heard the noise of coal being shovelled, then we saw her pick up a bucket and go inside again.

"So she's using it too," said Lizzie. "And look, so's Mrs Hipkin, look, there she is. What do you bet they'll be complaining about everybody else doing it tomorrow."

"Yes. But I should think they're as cold as the rest of us. Anyway I'm going out to have a look for myself. Leslie and Lily you dare move, you know what our Mum would say if you were out this late, crash or no crash."

But I couldn't stop Lizzie, we were both of us gone before Mum noticed. She was in the kitchen anyway now, we could hear her, the fire in the front room leaping up nicely all by itself as Mum's fires always did. "You ought to be my steam-raiser as well my missus," our Dad had used to say to her fondly in our happier days.

I could have done without Lizzie. I wanted to go by myself, to look by myself. It's one of the problems of being almost the eldest in a family, you're always answering questions, the Mum and Dad kind like: "Where've you been?", "What have you been up to?", "Why do you look such a mess?", and the rest of them from the kids almost always beginning "Why?". Fortunately, Lizzie didn't have much to say that evening. The street was full of people hurrying like us to get round the corner of Mrs Buttress's shop. She was standing at the door, her arms folded, the light behind her showing the pyramids of tins and packets, the bags of biscuits and sugar and beans, the jars of toffee and barley sugar which looked such plenty but had to be divided among so many. Her dog was shut in the room behind, you could hear it scratching at the door and whining and barking, while Mrs B. herself was telling anyone who would listen how wicked it all was, how she'd seen it coming, how

she'd seen it all happening with her own eyes, looking out of her upstairs window she had been, just by chance, she thought the whole train was going to land on top of her; how she'd sent for the police herself and the ambulance. That was another thing about Mrs B., she had the only telephone in our street.

Beyond her, down as far as the railway bridge and under it, the whole road had turned into a coal heap with a couple of smashed-up trucks lying on top, as if someone had thrown them there casually. There were no police there yet, nor ambulances, just people, almost all of them from Kirtley Villas, staring and arguing. Mr Bean the stationmaster arrived suddenly and started to tell everyone to stand back please in a loud voice; but no one did; there was not much point in it. The road was already well and truly blocked. And up on the line itself the lights walked to and fro; Dad, I thought, among others.

The ground was all covered in snow, the new as trampled by now as the old. But there was no snow on top of the tumbled coal, it must have stopped falling as if by magic straight after the crash.

"Lucky no one was in the street," a voice said behind me, "when that lot came down." I turned and found Beryl—she used to be my best friend when we were both at the juniors, but she's at the secondary modern now, though everyone expected her to get to the grammar with me, so I don't see so much of her these days. She was with her brother Chris, but before I'd had time to say hullo there was a loud ring-

ing way behind us and a police car came tearing up the street, making everyone scatter very fast, including me. They screeched to a halt and two officers got out and started talking to Mr Bean about getting the road cleared. A whole lot of people crowded round them arguing and trying to explain what had happened. I saw Beryl's dad and Mr Marwick back from his

billiards and Mr Potter, not drunk for once, and four of his sad and scruffy kids.

"Got to get the road cleared" someone said again, very loudly. Chris and Beryl's dad was sending them home for shovels and buckets, soon everyone was offering to help and some people miraculously had shovels already, that grated loudly on the coal as they began to dig. I decided I would go home for a shovel too. But then I saw Joe go past me with ours, and at the same time lights came walking down the steps from the signal box up on the embankment, and behind one of the lights was our Dad.

"Better go and tell Mum," I said to Lizzie. The scene was beginning to look like a party, I didn't want to have to leave yet. On the other hand, Dad might be bringing one of the drivers home and we might be able to hear what happened. Two more police cars arrived with their bells ringing loudly as I turned the corner.

The fire in the front room was beautiful now, all tall flames leaping. I don't think you can know how good a fire is until you've had to try and live without it. I think being warm is one of the nicest and most important things I know. But I wasn't given any time to enjoy it because Mum was fussing round and sending me to find teaspoons and things like that, and in between whiles asking me where I'd been, as if there was anything surprising in my wanting to go out and see it all for myself. And the next moment Dad had come in and two other men in peaked caps and dirty overalls with very grimy faces, who made our front room look tiny; or maybe our tiny front room simply made them look big. And there was Mum with her tray and the teapot on it steaming— our largest teapot. How about our tea ration? I thought rather sourly; and worse still, our cake tin with the precious cake that she'd saved up our rations for weeks? Why couldn't they drink their own tea, I thought? Why couldn't they eat their own cake? Both the men had brought their tea-cans in. Mum needn't have bothered to find cups.

I must say they did look pretty shaken up and frightened. One of them, Nocker, was an old mate of Dad's, he'd been in the pilot engine, the one in front; the other was a bloke from Derby Dad hadn't come across before. They gulped their tea down thankfully, and as for the cake they ate it in such great bites they can hardly have tasted it—what a dreadful waste! Mum didn't offer Lizzie and me any cake either, though we stared at it hard enough. She just stared back at us meaningfully, so we knew that was the end of it.

"What about your firemen then?" she asked Nocker and his mate.

Nocker said his fireman had been scalded but not badly, he'd stayed up on the footplate to wait for the ambulance and the second fireman was looking after him. "They're all right," he said.

"I know they're not," said Mum. "I'd better take them up some tea as well, and some bread-and-dripping." Well, at least there might be *some* cake left for us, I thought.

"All right, I'll go," Dad said. "I'll take my tea can." He put on his donkey jacket and railway cap and off he went again, with me this time, though I didn't ask if I could go in case he said no. There were more people in the street now than ever; people with shovels and buckets and coal hods and wheelbarrows, the police directing them; three police cars but still no ambulance; people not simply digging but also walking off with buckets of coal and the police taking no notice at all. They weren't interested in anything except clearing the road.

Dad and I crossed over, went along the embankment a little way and climbed the wooden steps up to the signal box, the whole scene gradually falling away below us, the cars and the people and the heaps of coal and the splintered trucks all caught in the thin yellow light of the two street lamps. We met another policeman on top. "Where do you think you're off to?" he asked, looking at me. But then he noticed Dad's railway cap and Dad waving the tea-can at him hardly needed to explain any more. "Wouldn't mind some of that myself," the policeman said. "What a night. We might as well go and live at the North Pole and be done with it."

We walked along the track to the foremost of the two engines, the pilot. It was still on the track, still hissing quietly; and we could see a faint glow from the fire on the footplate. But its tender was derailed, so was the big engine behind and its tender. The two men sitting on the pilot's footplate looked done-in, though they brightened up considerably at the sight of us and the tea-can. One of them had his arm roughly bandaged. "That ambulance is taking its time," he said.

"Cheer up, mate. I tell you, you're going to live,"

said the other. And then to Dad, "Is that your daughter then?"

"That's right; my eldest, Rosie."

"Two kinds of rosie you brought us then," said the fireman, winking at me. "What a night, eh? I wouldn't go through this again in a hurry." Of all of them I'd seen he was the only one who didn't look absolutely terrified. He took great swigs from the lid of the tea-can and said "That's a bit of all right then. That's what I needed."

I always like the footplates of engines. Even that night I liked that footplate; that tiny space with its smell of soot and hot metal; I like the smell and echo of the metal, I particularly like the hopeful glow of the fire. It makes me think of the fire that's supposed to be at the centre of the earth that none of us will ever see. I like the way at night your eyes get as if drawn into the small but brilliant heart of the fire, while outside there is such gloom and obscurity. It'll be a shame, I think, when all the trains are driven by other means than steam. Electric trains won't be nearly so exciting, so alive; steam engines are like animals, it's as if they could at any minute leap out at you and bite. Dad says though it'll be the best day of his life if he's ever put on an electric train; you won't get smuts in your eyes on electric trains, you won't sweat from the fire in front and freeze from the wind behind, you won't burn yourself every time you touch a bit of metal by mistake, without cotton waste round your fingers. I wouldn't know about that. I only know how it was that night and other nights for me; with the smell of the engine grease, the hiss from the dying steam, the hot orange glow of the fire; and those tired men sitting there, slumped down and drinking tea.

We heard another bell then from the street. "This time it must be the ambulance," said Dad. And he sent me off to tell the ambulance men where to come.

"Though I bet they know," I said. And then I was to go straight home and not hang about in the street; which I did, rather reluctantly, everyone else I knew being out there. But about five minutes later Dad reappeared himself and with him this time one of the Tailend Charlies, a pale-faced and runny-nosed bloke in a huge black coat, hung about like all guards with great bundles of flags and bags and lamps, and of course his tea-can. He was shaking with fright even more than the rest of them, and Mum became all motherly, she filled his tea-can to the very brim and gave him a huge slice of our by now fast dwindling cake. He told us his mate had gone back up the track placing detonators to warn any train coming along behind; he was now in the signal box getting warm on the signal man's tea.

"Why couldn't they all get warm on railway tea?" Lizzie whispered, nudging me furiously. If you only knew what it was like having so little for ourselves, maybe you'd understand why we sounded so mean about our tea and cake.

Pretty soon the men all began arguing about what could have happened. No one seemed to know exactly. Dad said they'd been going pretty fast from what he could hear, and Nocker in the pilot said it had been a blinding snow-storm, he couldn't see much, he might have overshot a signal, he hoped not. But their coal had been of such shocking quality and wet into the bargain, they'd been having trouble with the steam and he'd been helping the fireman. While the Derby man said he couldn't see anything either because of the snow and because of all the steam and smoke that was bearing down on him from the pilot. "*And* it's the first coal train through for a fortnight," he said gloomily. "There's going to be trouble for someone I tell you, whatever happens."

After what had happened to Dad last summer I could imagine it. I didn't want to listen any more, so when Mum's back was turned I slipped out again to see what was happening.

I've never seen so many people down our street before; people with handcarts and barrows, with buckets and baths and coal hods, people with spades and shovels long-handled and short-handled, the whole district by now must know what was happening. One bit of the road was almost cleared already. I saw Mr Blackie, the totter, with his horse and cart, making his way through. "Had to give 'em a hand, didn't I?" he was saying to anyone who would listen. "Thought me and Nobby here could shift quite a tidy bit for 'em." But I don't doubt either, that quite a lot of the coal stuck to his cart in the process.

Mr Bean, the station-master, was still fussing around, but with him now, to my surprise, was his son Billy, without his blue school cap and looking as lively as I'd ever seen him. I wondered how he'd escaped his mum. But the next person I saw was Mrs Buttress herself talking to a man in a coat with big shoulders and a sharp hat pulled down well over his eyes; definitely a spiv; and any spiv Mrs B. talked to had to be none other than her nephew Albert.

"Watch out," I said to Beryl who'd just come up to me, followed by Jean and Peggy, two of the thin and dirty Potter girls whom she'd taken in hand recently for reasons of her own. "Watch out," I said. "Didn't you see that Albert, the spiv? He must think there's something in this for him. Sell the lot on the Black Market he would, given half a chance."

"Do you really think he will?" said Beryl, breathlessly.

"I daresay, if there's any left." I was watching Mr Potter direct two of Jean and Peggy's brothers to carry off a large bucket-load each; though I must say there was so much coal there still it was hard to believe any had been shifted at all.

"But *Albert*," Beryl was saying. "We'll have to stop him."

"Oh come off it, Beryl, how could we stop anyone. I only said he might. I was joking mostly."

"I'm not joking. I will stop him."

"Rather you than me. Oh come on, Beryl, it is a joke."

Beryl really is astonishing. Half the time she moons about gloomily chewing something or other (though goodness knows what she found to chew those days). It's obvious why she's so fat. You can speak to her then and she doesn't hear a word you're saying, she's in such a state of dream. Then all at once it's as if someone lit a fire in her like in an engine, and she starts blowing out such steam, such energy, Lord help anyone who gets in her way. I wasn't going to, I decided. And if Albert did . . . well, it'd be one in the eye for Mrs Buttress. But I didn't take any of it very seriously. I watched a bit longer while they cleared a path through the coal big enough for one of the police cars to get through, throwing the coal up against the hoarding on the far side of the road until the tiny poster in the middle of it was entirely hidden. I caught sight of my brother Joe shovelling too, but he was with three of his mates.

They were having a high old time and it looked more like a kind of game to me.

I was frozen to my bones by this time and pretty tired too, so I went straight up to him and got him to come home with me, though protesting loudly. The Tailend Charlie had left our front room but the drivers were still there and a couple of policemen besides. The room was full of smoke and two-thirds of our precious cake had vanished. As for our tea ration . . . it didn't look to me as if we could afford to get on the wrong side of Mrs Buttress for some time to come. But oh how warm the room was! I don't believe our front room had been so cosy for years and years.

I woke in the night very suddenly. Lizzie had tugged the sheets away from me. "Wake *up*, Rosie. Wake *up*, will you."

"What's the matter?"

"Beryl's outside throwing things up at the window. She says we're to come out. She'll have woken Leslie and Lily in a minute, and Mum and Dad before we know where we are, and then there'll be trouble. Do get up, Rosie."

Sighing I put my clothes on. I knew just the sort of mood Beryl was in; and this time there was no getting out of her way. Lizzie insisted on coming with me, but the twins were still asleep and so, thank goodness, was Joe, lying on his back with his mouth open.

34

"Come on," hissed Beryl, when we joined her. "How could you take so *long*? It's him, Albert. He's back with his lorry, like you said. We've got to stop him, all of us."

She had Chris with her and one of her sisters, Molly, and Michael and Eric the two boys from next door. She also, more surprisingly, had Jean and Peggy, the one defiant, the other terrified—as always; (for Jean had run away from home twice, and once been put into a children's home; whereas Peggy, at a guess, does half their mother's work). She was no taller than Jean, though two years older, and looked so pale and tired and so scared all the time, just as she did now. The last person Beryl had brought did not look scared though; he was the most surprising of all; I stared at him in amazement; Billy Bean the station-master's son.

"What did you have to bring him for?" I whispered to Beryl as we walked along behind the rest of them. "What good's he going to be, for heaven's sake?"

"There's nothing wrong with him except his mum. And that goes for a lot of people," she said, looking at Peggy and Jean. "Anyway, he said he wanted to come. I asked him earlier."

"But if his mum. . . ."

"Who's afraid of the big bad wolf? *Mothers.* You can keep them."

"There's nothing wrong with my mum, Beryl Jelly."

"Never said there was. Now come on. Quiet everyone, we don't want to warn them we're coming."

We crept up to the corner by Mrs Buttress's shop and put our heads round it very cautiously. There was Albert's lorry and another one beyond the coal heap in the shadow of the bridge and a third beyond that. This belonged to Phipps the coal merchant, I didn't know about the other one. There were two men with full coal sacks heading towards these and two more men shovelling. Albert wasn't shovelling, of course, or carrying. He wasn't going to spoil his fancy suit with coal, not him, he stood directing everyone else instead.

"Well the first thing is to ring the police," said Beryl.

"The police? What will they do? They weren't stopping anyone earlier."

"But this is different. This is large-scale robbery. They're gangsters. We've got to ring the police."

We were standing right beside Mrs Buttress's neat little blue notice which said 'You may telephone from here'; in spite of which notice she would often tell people it was inconvenient, so that they would have to trail off to the phone box three-quarters of a mile down the road; another reason for keeping on the right side of Mrs Buttress. It was hardly likely to be convenient now. Anyway I couldn't see myself asking her if I could use her phone to set the police against her Albert, especially since she'd probably put him up to it in the first place. So it would have to be the phone box; and I had a shrewd idea it wasn't going to be Beryl who would have to walk all the way down there at two o'clock in the morning.

"You'd better go, Rosie," said Beryl, sure enough. "I ought to stay here, but it's got to be someone sensible."

"Thanks for the compliment. And what will you be doing in the meantime?"

"Distracting them; to stop them leaving before the police come."

"And how do you think you're going to manage that?"

"I'll think of something," said Beryl and I didn't doubt it, amazed all over again that it was me got into the grammar and not her—she is far more likely to end up Manageress of the International Stores than I am. Or else she's going to be an actress, I thought, watching her put on a prize-winning performance as our local spy, peering round the corner and ducking back again, a finger on her lips.

"You realise," I said, "I'm going to have to get past that lot without them seeing me. How am I supposed to do that?"

"You don't have to worry about a *thing*," said Beryl. "You just watch me." She beckoned imperiously to Lizzie and Eric and Michael and Jean and Peggy and Molly and Chris, and to Billy who was standing a little away from the others looking awkward. Then she advanced round the corner boldly, the rest of them trailing after her rather more uncertainly. She marched straight up to Albert the Spiv and started to say something. I didn't hear what because I took my chance and sneaked down towards the gap through the coal under the bridge, between the side of a lorry and the cold and grimy brick and was away down the street, slipping and skidding on the snow, the soft new layer on top hiding a hard and treacherous layer of ice beneath.

The phone box smelt cold and stale as it always did. I picked up the receiver and waited for the operator to say number please. It felt as if I had stood there for five minutes before the voice finally came.

"Police," I said. "And hurry. They'll get away if you don't." I forgot she couldn't know what I was talking about. My breath made huge visible gusts in the air. I was panting suddenly very hard, as much from a sudden rush of anxiety as from the effort of skidding half-a-mile. My hands and feet all ached with cold, particularly my feet. My shoes were useless for keeping out the snow—even if Mum could have spared the coupons and the cash to buy me a pair of warm boots I doubt if she'd have found any in the shops. So I stamped my feet and waited yet again.

All the burglars in the world could have escaped, it seemed to me, before another voice answered, a man's this time. "Police Station," it said.

"That coal," I said, "from the accident on the railway by Railway Approach; you *know*; there's blokes there with lorries; if you don't come quick they'll have pinched the lot."

"Now then, now then," said the voice at the other end. "Say all that again, slowly, if you don't mind. Now then, *coal* did you say?"

I explained it all over again. Even then I was made to repeat some of it twice.

"It won't be a matter of coal," I said bitterly, "if you don't come quick, there won't be any coal left."

"That's enough of that then, laddy. What did you say your name was?"

"I didn't," I said, not sure whether I found being called laddy a compliment or not. But I'd had enough of all this by now. "Do hurry. Just come," I said and slammed the phone down.

Then I went back up the road again cold and cross and agitated too. Surely Albert and the rest would have taken alarm and disappeared by now.

But I heard them long before I reached the bridge. Voices shouting and others singing; children's voices and behind them men's, these very angry. I slid back under the bridge wondering whatever I was going to find. I came under the street lamp on the other side and saw them all and could hardly believe my eyes. There were far more children there than when I left,

Beryl must somehow have knocked up the entire street. There were all the Potters, for instance, even the baby, carried by Peggy, naturally, and wailing loudly, and all Beryl's brothers, and the noisy Marwick children from next door, there was Joe and, heavens above, Leslie and Lily too, on top of the coal, on top of the lorries, all of them dancing around and singing at the tops of their voices or else shouting insults such as "Yah-boo, Fat-Face, Spiv-Head, Big-Nose, *Thief*." The Marwick children from next door were loudest of anyone of course, they'd had plenty of practice; though I don't imagine they had actually been encouraged to make such a noise before. 'Roll out the Barrel' I heard someone singing; and then suddenly I heard Beryl.

"Let him go," she was singing, "Let him go let him tarry, let him sink or let him swim, he does not care for me, and I don't care for *him*."

She was standing on the bonnet of Albert's lorry waving her arms as if she was conducting everybody else. "He does not care for me, and I don't care for *him*." And behind and above her peering out of her upstairs window was Mrs Buttress herself in curlers, and beyond her the backs of Kirtley Villas sprouted more heads, both Marwicks, both Sprotts, and Mrs Hipkin, Mum and Beryl's mum and Mrs Potter. And there was Albert trying to get back into his lorry and get it started, only there were children climbing all over it now so he couldn't, and he was shouting words none of us were supposed to know but of course we all did. Then suddenly round the corner came our Dad and Beryl's dad, and Mr Potter and Mr Bean the station-master and Mrs Bean the station-master's wife saying "Where's my Billy—where's my Billy?" while there was her Billy having the time of his life dancing about on a heap of coal sacks and yelling "Death to the French" for some reason, in a very high voice. At which moment too came a great ringing of bells and down the street tore not one but two police cars and screeched to a halt in front of us. So they had taken me seriously after all.

And no one ended up buying that coal on the Black Market. Albert was charged with trying to rob the railway company and got six months inside, as did Mr Phipps the coal merchant. But I don't think anyone in the streets round us died of cold that winter. Of course the railway came and removed the coal from the street and the embankment and out of our back yards, but we all had full coal bunkers and no one seemed to grudge us that, and until they had cleared it away they didn't seem to grudge any locals the odd bucket or two either, or rather they just turned a blind eye to it. The broken waggons chopped up made splendid firewood. It got us through the winter, the whole excitement I mean, as well as the wood and the coal. You cannot imagine how endless and dreary and uncomfortable it would have seemed otherwise.

It was Beryl—of course—who suggested that it ought to be celebrated properly; what had happened; and Beryl also who suggested how it should be celebrated. At the end of the war, on VE Day, we'd had a party in Railway Approach, the whole street had joined in. We'd set up trestle tables in the road and had a feast, and then we'd danced all evening. Why didn't we do that again, Beryl said, to celebrate the coal? To celebrate the end of winter even. For almost overnight, round about May the first, the weather had changed, the sun shone every day, it was beautiful.

The grown-ups were very doubtful at first, but then someone took the idea up, it might even have been my Dad, I don't remember, and whoever it was gradually managed to convince everyone. Why shouldn't we have a party? We could all do with cheering up the way things dragged on and on; because rationing was as bad as ever. So everyone saved up their coupons for a month and made cakes and biscuits, besides that we had jam sandwiches and potted meat sandwiches and egg sandwiches, the eggs coming from chickens kept by friends of Mrs Hipkin in the country; which was nice of her, she could have kept the eggs and eaten them all herself. There was lemonade for the children and tea for the grown-ups and later on some beer from the pub. And Mr Sprott brought out his gramophone and records, mostly from before the war, band records, Ambrose and Glenn Miller and Victor Sylvester, and everyone danced. In between whiles we had a sing-song, all the old favourites, 'Roll Out the Barrel' and 'Oh, Oh, Antonio' and 'My Old Man' and 'Run Rabbit Run' and 'Kiss Me Goodnight, Sergeant Major'; and of course 'Let Him Go Let Him Tarry'. Beryl sang that solo because she really was the heroine of the evening.

But everyone was cheerful. The Potter kids even looked clean, for them, and the Marwick kids only fought once and their Dad separated them and spoke to them sternly and they didn't try it again. Mrs Sprott and Mrs Hipkin didn't dance, they sat on two easy chairs brought out from our house and gossiped to each other, about the rest of us no doubt, but they looked quite kindly. Even Mrs Buttress came and stood at her door and watched in spite of her Albert getting into trouble. And she brought out a whole jar of liquorice allsorts to give the children; they were a bit stale but no one was complaining, except her dog, which rushed round barking at everyone till she shut him at the back of her shop.

I suppose the biggest surprise though was Billy Bean who dressed up as Charlie Chaplin and did a turn that made us all laugh, he's a real comedian that boy. He still has to wear his little blue cap to school, but since that night his mother hasn't been able to stop him coming out with the rest of us, it's all made more difference to him than anyone.

I'll tell you who else came to our party; my brother Alan home on leave from Germany, and also Dad's mate Nocker who'd been driving the pilot train that night. I don't know that he felt that happy about it all; he'd been cleared of the blame for the accident by the inquiry, as far as the inquiry could judge the points had been wrong not the drivers, they'd frozen solid, that's why the train jumped. Still an accident never does your record any good and for the time

being he'd been put on shunting with Dad. Still, he said he was glad about the coal for us, and free beer suited him any time. I said Dad should have invited the fireman and the Tailend Charlie too but Dad said that wouldn't do at all. They are such snobs, railwaymen, it's worse than school, teachers looking down on pupils, sixth form on fourth form and so on.

I don't think anything was ever quite as bad again. 1948 was a pretty cold winter too, but nothing was quite as short as it had been the year before; and afterwards slowly conditions began to improve. It was worth losing our rations that night, I decided.

(Anyway Lizzie and Joe and Leslie and Lily and I had been allowed to finish the cake up after all. Mum had scolded us for going out, but in the end she had said she was proud of us and we deserved it; and anyway it was hardly worth leaving what was left of it now. So we had sat in front of the fire drinking tea and eating cake and having the time of our lives at three in the morning, think of it. And all because the coal train came down the hill in a snow storm and fell off the railway track.)

# Long Ago Children Books: complete list of titles